Garby
The Garbage Truck

Written and designed by Tamara Berk

ISBN 9781521762479

Garby the **green** garbage truck lived in a big city called Wallisville.

Every Tuesday, Garby drove all over the city and collected *smelly* garbage.

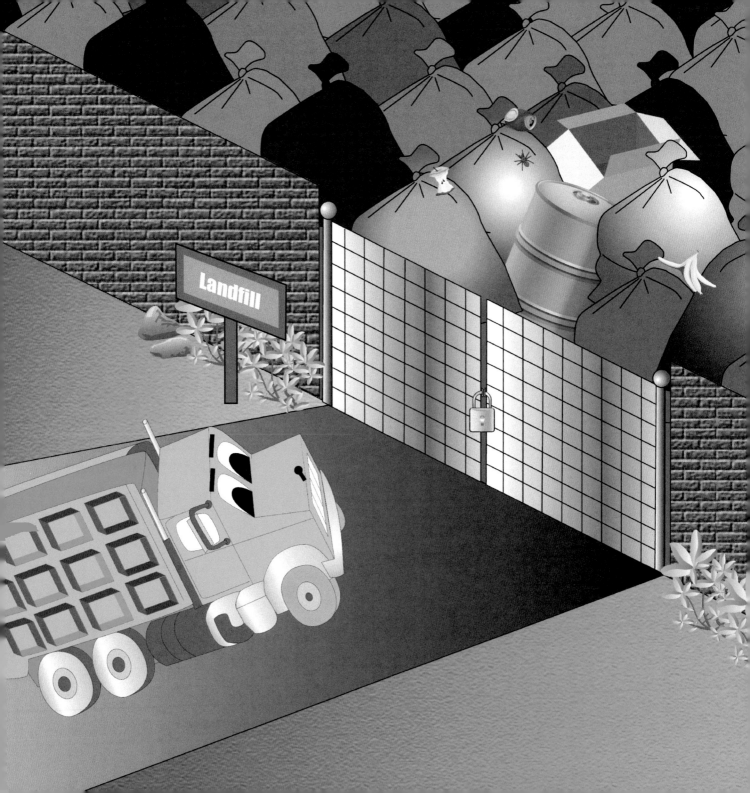

Garby would take all the garbage to the landfill, but one day, the gates were locked and he couldn't get inside. The landfill was **full**!

Garby had to find somewhere else to put the garbage, but he wasn't sure where. So he drove away in search of another place.

As Garby drove down the street, he hit a bump in the road causing one of the garbage bags to roll onto the grass and **smash** open.

When he went to clean it up, he noticed glass bottles inside, and these could be returned to the store.

Garby had an 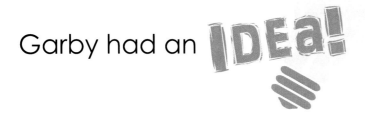 IDEa!

He would open all bags and find new places to put everything, because it wasn't really garbage after all.

He hoped no more *smelly* landfills would be made, and instead the land would be used for parks.

The next Tuesday, Garby was so **excited** to sort through all the garbage and make sure that it didn't end up in a landfill.

Now, Garby didn't want to be a **green** garbage truck; instead, he wanted to be a **blue** recycling truck.

Garby was so happy to start his new job as
a recycling truck and save the world from
smelly landfills!

Eco-friendly tips for you and your family

1. Remember to turn off anything that can be turned on, when you don't need it.

2. Use reusable and washable containers and bags that don't need to be thrown out.

3. Share with your family and friends. Many items, such as books, magazines, movies, games, and newspapers can be used by more than one person.

4. Lots of items can go into the compost or organic waste, such as left over food, paper towels and diapers.

5. There are many ways to save water, such as turning off the faucet when you're brushing your teeth or the shower when you're shampooing your hair.

6. Visit your local zoo and aquarium and learn more about how you, your family and friends can help the environment.

Manufactured by Amazon.ca
Bolton, ON

15479508R00017